ADVENTURE AHEAD

TRAINING RAPTORS IS JUST LIKE TRAINING DOGS. HEEL! SIT! FETCH!

WHY IS THE GROUND SHAKING?

HAS ANYONE LOST A DINOSAUR?

I'LL DESTROY THIS PARK!

TWO OF A KIND
Can you spot the two identical ACU guards?

LET'S RIDE!

LOOK! A TREASURE MAP!

DID SOMEBODY SAY TREASURE?

NOW I CAN SEE IN THE DARK!

LET'S TAKE THE DINOMECH OUT FOR A SPIN

FANCY A SNACK?

TIME FOR SOME TREASURE HUNTING

BEST THEME PARK EVER!

BLUE, DELTA, ECHO, CHARLIE ...

... ALL PRESENT!

WHO LIKES GETTING THEIR NOSE TICKLED?

RIVER RAPIDS

Guide the dinghy through the river maze to lead Owen and Claire to the treasure.

THE RAPTOR BABIES ARE GETTING BIGGER EVERY DAY

AN EGG-CITING SURPRISE!

QUICK DRAW

Fill in the empty squares in the bottom picture to complete the drawing of Blue.

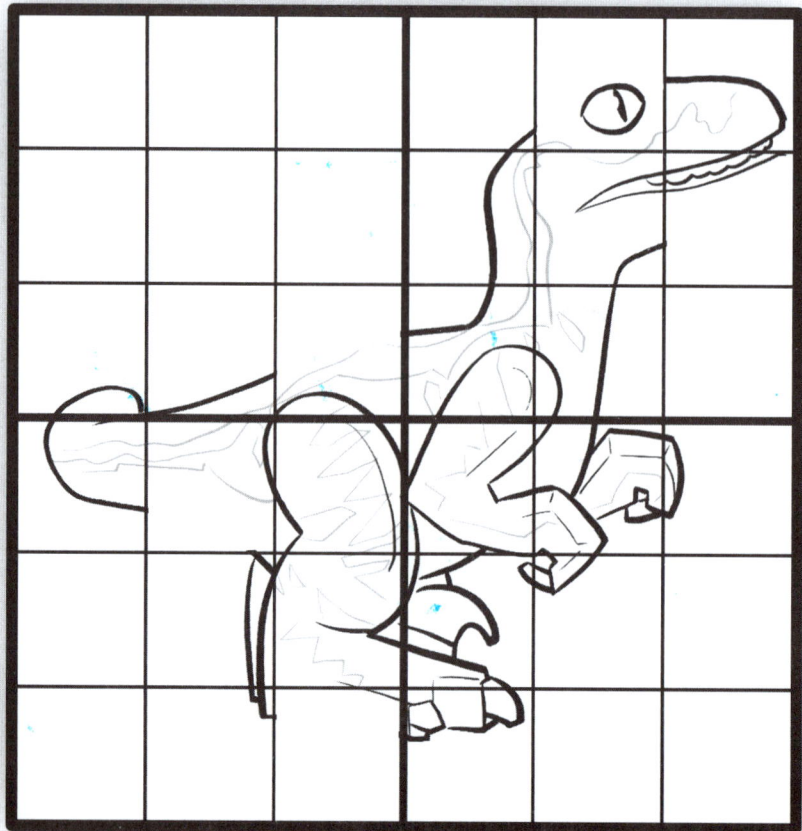

STIGGY WANTS A CARROT

THIS IS A GREAT SPOT FOR FISHING ...

... BUT NOT FOR SWIMMING!

FETCH!

SO MUCH TREASURE!

CAN YOU SPOT THE EXTRA PASSENGER ON BOARD?

CLEAN-UP CONUNDRUM
Can you find the one item that is not part of a pair?

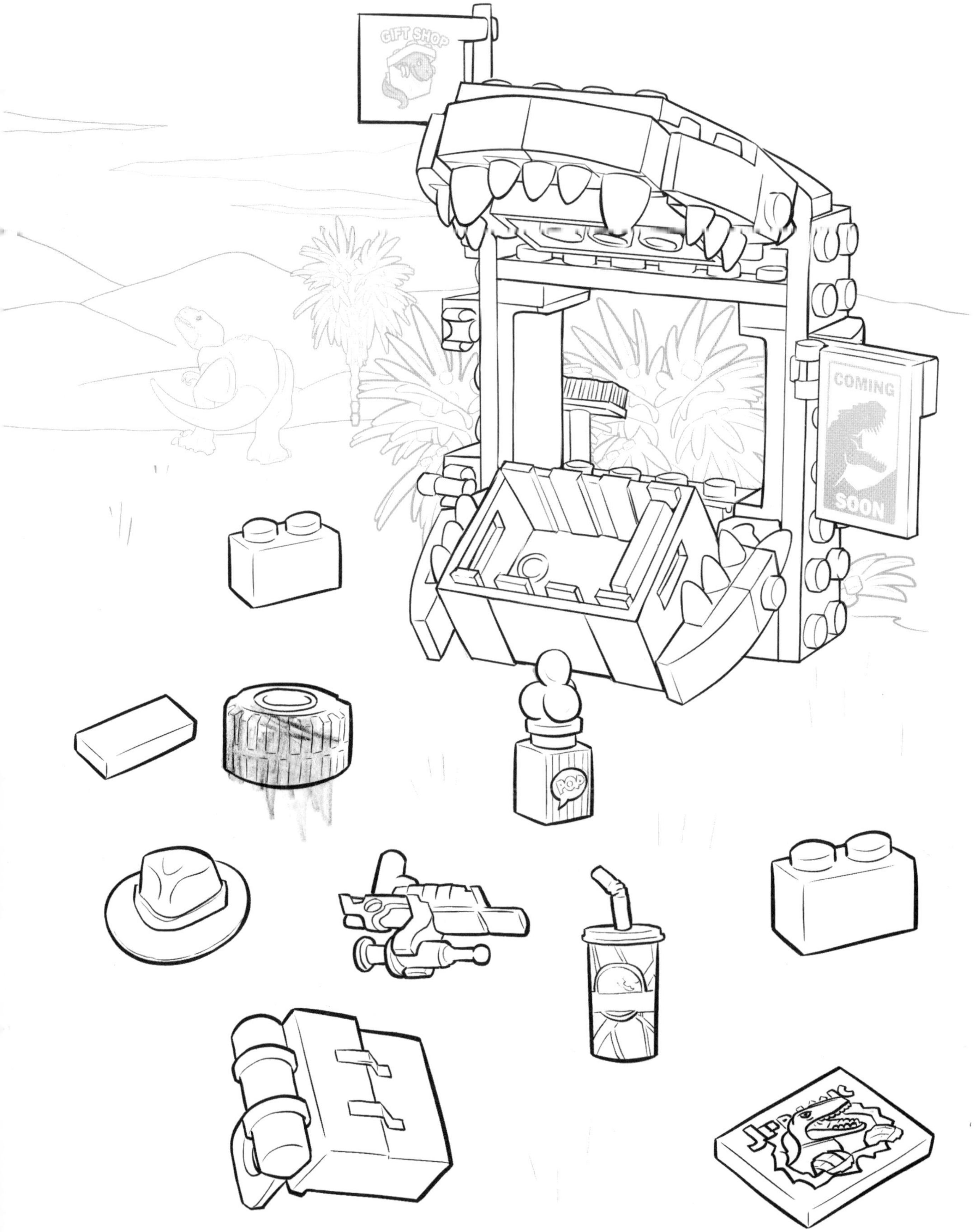
GIFT SHOP
COMING
SOON
POP

WELCOME TO THE PARK!

CAN ANYONE SMELL BREAKFAST?

DELTA'S GETTING HUNGRY!

FINDING RAPTORS TAKES AN EXPERT TRACKER

WHO'S A GOOD BABY?

THIS ONE SURE IS THIRSTY!

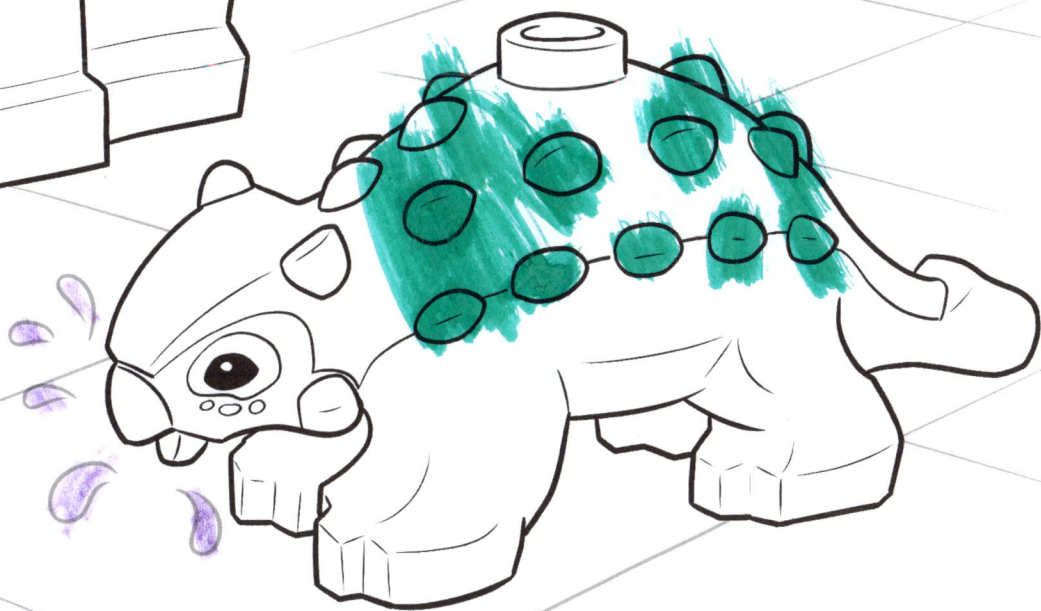

LET LOOSE

Five small dinosaurs are hiding in this crowd. Can you find them?

NEW ARRIVAL
Draw and colour the baby dinosaur that has just hatched.

WHERE ARE THE BRAKES ON THIS THING?

ROAR!

TIME TO STRETCH THOSE WINGS

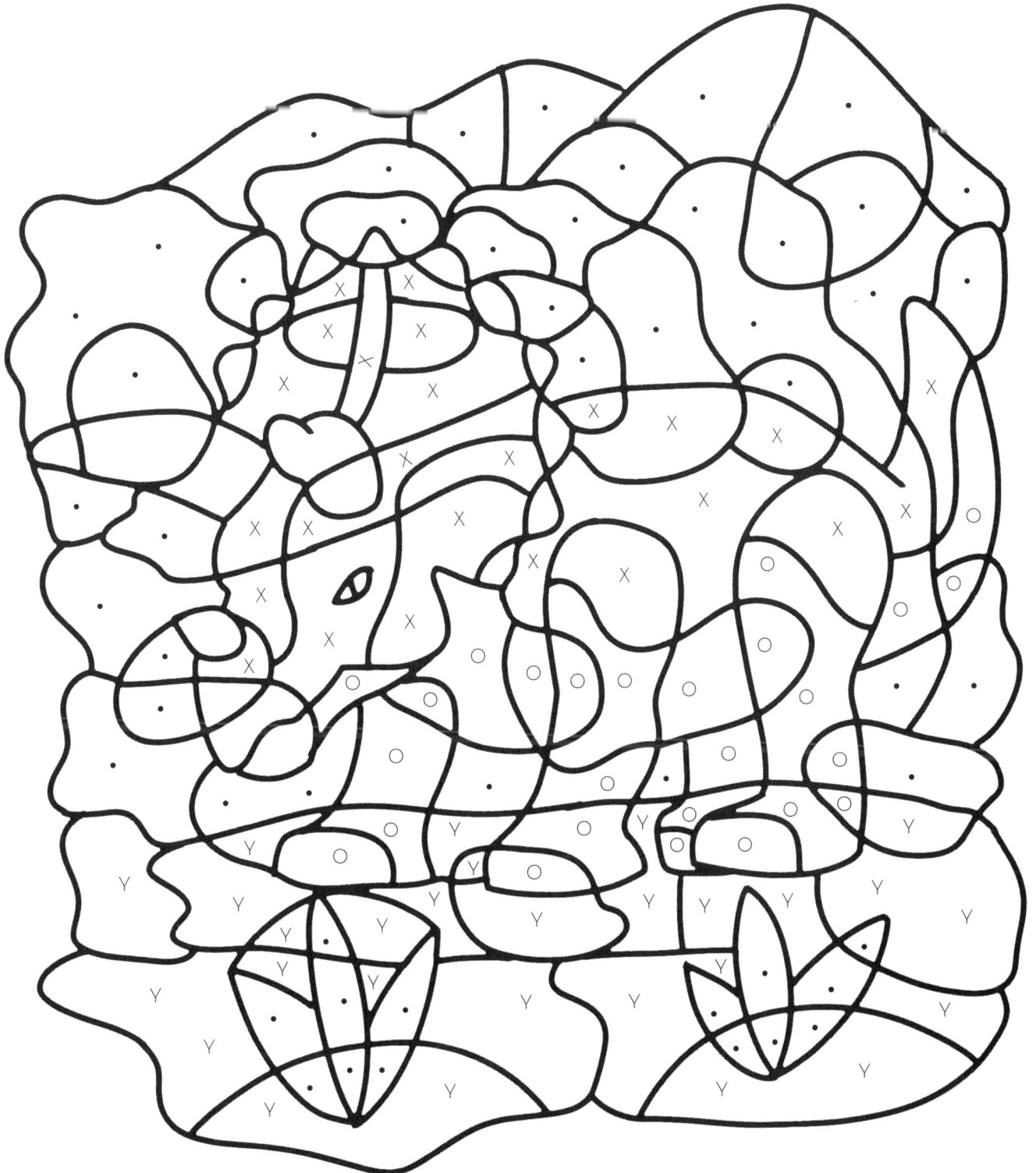

COLOUR CODES

Use the code to colour the picture and find out who's hiding on this page.

• – GREEN   X – BROWN   O – ORANGE   Y – YELLOW

COME IN, PATROL! DO YOU COPY?

WE'RE RIGHT HERE!

SOMEONE'S IN A BAD MOOD

CARNOTAURUS APPROACHING!

ANSWERS

p. 6

p. 19

p. 30–31

p. 38

p. 43

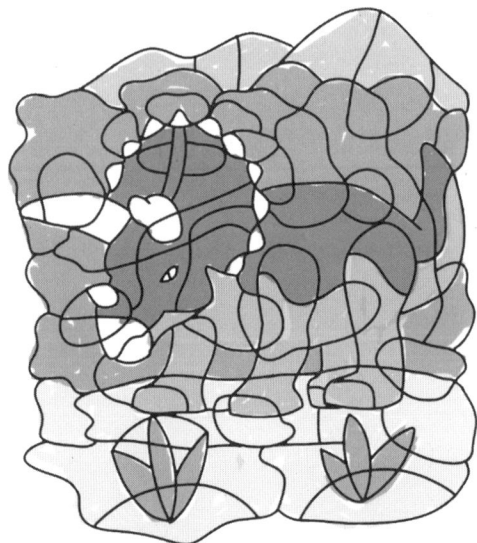